Please, Mr Magic Fish!

Jessica Souhami

Otter-Barry BOOKS

One amazing day, fisherman Jack caught an unusual fish. He was just about to put it in his bag when the fish spoke.

"Jack," it said. "I'm a magic fish. If you free me I'll grant your dearest wish."

Jack was astounded. He let the fish slip back
into the sea and hurried home in a daze.

"Liz," he said to his wife, "you'll never guess
in a million years what's just happened!"

Jack told her all about the magic fish.

"And you didn't think to make a wish," said Liz,
"when we live in a cold hut with holes in the roof
and barely enough to eat? You **dunderhead!**"

"Oh, you're right, Liz," said Jack.
"Let's go and find the fish right now."

So Jack and Liz hurried to the shore and called out,
"Please, Mr Magic Fish, will you grant our dearest wish?"

The fish rose up from the calm green sea.
"What is your wish?" it said.

"Please may we have a small dry cottage?" said Jack.

"And a blue teapot?" said Liz.

"And some bread and cheese in the larder?" added Jack.

"Certainly," said the fish.

"Turn around, turn around and see what you will see. "

"Thank you. Thank you so much," they called.

And there was the prettiest little cottage.
It had flowers in the front
and vegetables at the back,
chickens in the yard,
bread and cheese in the larder,
and a blue teapot on the table.

And they were happy for a month.

But then Liz said, "The rooms are very small and very plain. Life here is dull."

"And the food is boring," added Jack. "Let's go to see the fish once more."

At the shore Jack and Liz called out,
"Please, **Mr Magic Fish, will you grant us one more wish?**"

The fish rose up from the choppy blue sea.
"What is your wish?" it said.

"Please may we have a large sunny house?" said Jack.

"With lace curtains and velvet cushions?" said Liz.

"And puddings and pies in the larder?" added Jack.

"Very well," said the fish. "Turn around, turn around and see what you will see."

"**Thanks**," they called.

And they turned around... and turned around . . .

And there was a handsome house
full of elegant furniture,
set in a big garden with fruit trees
and flowers of every kind.
There were lace curtains and velvet cushions,
and puddings and pies in the larder.

And Jack and Liz were happy for a week.

But then Liz said, "Now we've come up
in the world this really isn't good enough.
We should live like a lord and lady in a palace."

"Yes," said Jack. "And the food should be fancier too!
Let's go back to the fish!"

Back at the shore Jack and Liz called out,
"Please, Mr Magic Fish, will you grant us one more wish?"

The fish rose up from the stormy purple sea.
"Yes?" it said.

"Please may we have a palace?" said Jack.

"With chandeliers and silver spoons?" said Liz.

"And jellies and trifles in the larder?" added Jack.

"All right," said the fish.

"Turn around, turn around and see what you will see. "

But they did **not** say thank you!

And they turned around... and turned around . . .

And there was a splendid palace with a hundred rooms,
stone columns, and marble floors.
It stood in vast grounds with beautiful gardens,
orchards and woods.
There were crystal chandeliers and silver spoons,
and jellies and trifles in the larder.

And they were happy for a day.

"We deserve better," said Liz. "We should be rulers over all the land and the sea."

"Quite right, Liz," said Jack.
"Let's talk to that fish now."

Once more they called the fish.
"Please, Mr Magic Fish, will you grant us one more wish?"

And the fish rose up from the boiling dark sea.
"What now?" it said.

"We want to be King and Queen of all the land and sea,"
said Jack and Liz together.

And they turned around... and turned around . . .

And, as if it had all been a foolish dream, they were back once more with their cold, leaky hut, raggedy clothes and bare larder!

But I wonder what happened next?

Jack and Liz never saw the magic fish again.

But I hope they caught lots of ordinary fish
to sell at the market. And that they gradually
became happy.

What do you think?